Dear Parents,

Welcome to the Scholastic Reader series. We have taken over 80 years of experience with teachers, parents, and children and put it into a program that is designed to match your child's interests and skills.

Level 1—Short sentences and stories made up of words kids can sound out using their phonics skills and words that are important to remember.

Level 2—Longer sentences and stories with words kids need to know and new "big" words that they will want to know.

Level 3—From sentences to paragraphs to longer stories, these books have large "chunks" of texts and are made up of a rich vocabulary.

Level 4—First chapter books with more words and fewer pictures.

It is important that children learn to read well enough to succeed in school and beyond. Here are ideas for reading this book with your child:

- Look at the book together. Encourage your child to read the title and make a prediction about the story.
- Read the book together. Encourage your child to sound out words when appropriate. When your child struggles, you can help by providing the word.
- Encourage your child to retell the story. This is a great way to check for comprehension.
- Have your child take the fluency test on the last page to check progress.

Scholastic Readers are designed to support your child's efforts to learn how to read at every age and every stage. Enjoy helping your child learn to read and love to read.

— **Francie Alexander**
  Chief Education Officer
  Scholastic Education

SUPERTWINS™
MEET THE DANGEROUS DINO-ROBOTS

BY **B.J. JAMES**
ILLUSTRATED BY **CHRIS DEMAREST**

For Preston
—B.J.J.

For Jack & Lucas
—C.D.

Text copyright © 2003 by Brian Masino.
Illustrations copyright © 2003 by Chris Demarest.
All rights reserved. Published by Scholastic Inc.
SCHOLASTIC, CARTWHEEL BOOKS, and associated logos are trademarks and/or registered trademarks of Scholastic Inc.

Library of Congress Cataloging-in-Publication Data
James, Brian.
  Supertwins meet the dangerous dino-robots / by B.J. James; illustrated by Chris Demarest.
    p. cm. — (Scholastic readers. Level 2) "Cartwheel Books."
Summary: While on a field trip to a museum, young twin superheroes Timmy and Tabby battle robotic dinosaurs controlled by a mad scientist who plans to take over the world.
  ISBN 0-439-46625-3 (pbk.)
  [1. Heroes—Fiction. 2. Twins—Fiction. 3. Brothers and sisters—Fiction. 4. Robots—Fiction.
5. Dinosaurs—Fiction. 6. Scientists—Fiction. 7. Science museums—Fiction.] I. Demarest, Chris L., ill. II. Title. III. Series.
PZ7.J153585Sv 2003
[Fic]—dc21
2003003864

10 9 8 7 6 5 4 3 2 1   03 04 05 06 07
Printed in the U.S.A. 23 • First printing, September 2003

Scholastic Reader — Level 2

SCHOLASTIC INC.

New York   Toronto   London   Auckland   Sydney
Mexico City   New Delhi   Hong Kong   Buenos Aires

Chapter 1

Our class was going to the museum.
We were almost there.
The bus drove up to the door.

"Stand in a straight line,"
said Mrs. Shelly.
Mrs. Shelly is our teacher.
She is the nicest teacher
in the whole first grade!

"I hope we see the dinosaurs first!"
I said to Tabby.
Dinosaurs are my favorite.

"I hope we see the unicorns first!"
Tabby said to me.
Unicorns are her favorite.

"But, Tabby," I said, "unicorns aren't real!"
"So what?" she said.

Sometimes having a twin sister is harder than saving the world!

First we saw airplanes and trains.

Then we saw knights and swords.

We saw lots of fun stuff.
But we didn't see dinosaurs.

Then I saw a sign.
It said: DINOSAUR GARDEN.
The sign pointed to the right.
I was happy, because guess what?
Our class turned right!

Inside, there were all kinds of dinosaurs.
"Cool!" I yelled, because the dinosaurs
were robots.

A funny man with big glasses
told us about the dinosaurs.
His name was
Professor Albert.

I looked around.

Then I looked through the wall.
Superheroes can do that.
I saw more Dino-Robots!
They did NOT look nice.

I tried to tell Tabby.
Tabby told me to be quiet.
Then Mrs. Shelly told me to be quiet.

But I had a bad feeling about those robots!

Chapter 2

The class went outside
to eat lunch.
I had peanut butter and jelly.
So did Tabby.
My mom says that twins always
eat the same thing.

But I wasn't hungry.
I kept thinking about the
Dino-Robots.
They looked like trouble.
Tabby and I had to check
them out.

"Can we go to the bathroom?"
Tabby and I asked Mrs. Shelly.
Mrs. Shelly wanted to know why
we both had to go.
"Because we're twins!" I said.

She let us go.
I am glad she believed me.
I didn't want to tell her that
we are superheroes!

"Look!" I shouted.

Tabby told me to whisper. "You have to be quiet in a museum," she said.

IN PROFESSOR ALBERT'S SECRET ROOM...

Professor Albert was talking to the robots.
There were zillions of them.

"Dear Dino-Robots," Professor Albert said, "TODAY WE TAKE OVER THE WORLD!"

The Dino-Robots cheered.

"Oh, no!" I said.
"They could mess up the whole city!"

"Not if we stop them!" Tabby said.

This was a job for the Supertwins!

The Dino-Robots came closer.
They had really BIG metal teeth!
They got really close.
Then…

Tabby smashed a Dino-Robot
with one punch!

Tabby flew into the air.
I flew up behind her.
The Dino-Robots tried to grab us.
We flew super fast!
They couldn't catch us.

We super-punched them one-by-one. Those robots were no match for the Supertwins!

"Over there!" Tabby said. "That bad professor is getting away!"

"You kids will never catch me!"
the professor said.

He flew through
a hole in the roof.
We followed.

"Not so fast!" I yelled.

Then we caught him.

"RATS!"
he said.

Tabby and I took
the professor all the way to jail.

"He won't build any
Dino-Robots here!"
I said.

"Did we forget something?" Tabby said.
"What?" I asked.
Then we thought about it.

SCHOOL!

Chapter 3

We flew back to the museum.
Lunch was almost over.
Tabby and I joined our class.

I told Tabby to tuck in her cape.
She ALWAYS forgets!

"There you are!" Mrs. Shelly said.

"Where have you two been?"
Mrs. Shelly asked.
I kept quiet.
Superhero stuff is secret.

"We stopped those mean Dino-Robots
from taking over the world!" Tabby said.
"We picked them up. Then we dropped them."

'Did you two touch the exhibits?"
Mrs. Shelly asked.

'Maybe a little," we answered.

Mrs. Shelly told us that was against the rules.

'We're sorry," we said.

Even superheroes have to follow the rules!

Fluency Fun

The words in each list below end in the same sounds.
Read the words in a list.
Read them again.
Read them faster.
Try to read all 15 words in one minute.

pay	**bunch**	**dew**
x-ray	**lunch**	**new**
play	**munch**	**blew**
stay	**punch**	**flew**
away	**scrunch**	**stew**

Look for these words in the story.

could   **favorite**   **because**

were   **whole**

Note to Parents:

According to *A Dictionary of Reading and Related Terms*, fluency is "the ability to read smoothly, easily, and readily with freedom from word-recognition problems." Fluency is necessary for good comprehension and enjoyable reading. The activities on this page include a speed drill and a sight-recognition drill. Speed drills build fluency because they help students rapidly recognize common syllables and spelling patterns in words, and they're fun! Sight-recognition drills help students smoothly and accurately recognize words. Practice these activities with your child to help him or her become a fluent reader.

—**Wiley Blevins,**
Reading Specialist